Unbeatable Beaks

Stephen R. Swinburne
illustrated by Joan Paley

Henry Holt and Company
New York

To my father, whose love of words rubbed off on me
—S. S.

For my daughter, Jennifer, a wonderful artist and my most valued critic
—J. P.

Henry Holt and Company, Inc., *Publishers since 1866*
115 West 18th Street, New York, New York 10011

Henry Holt is a registered trademark of Henry Holt and Company, Inc.
Text copyright © 1999 by Stephen R. Swinburne. Illustrations copyright © 1999 by Joan Paley.
Published in Canada by Fitzhenry & Whiteside Ltd., 195 Allstate Parkway, Markham, Ontario L3R 4T8.

Library of Congress Cataloging-in-Publication Data
Swinburne, Stephen R.
Unbeatable beaks / by Stephen Swinburne; illustrated by Joan
Paley.
Summary: Rhyming verses describe many types of bird beaks.
Includes factual information about thirty-nine birds.
1. Bill (Anatomy)—Juvenile literature. [1. Bill (Anatomy). 2. Birds.]
I. Paley, Joan, ill. II. Title.
QL697.S85 1999 598.14—dc21 98-43348

ISBN 0-8050-4802-2 / First Edition—1999
Typography by Martha Rago
The artist used colored papers, paints, crayons,
and pencils to create the collages for this book.
Printed in Italy
10 9 8 7 6 5 4 3 2 1

Author's Note

I'm always looking at birds. On my walks to the post office, I keep an eye out for Baltimore orioles nesting in a big poplar tree along the river. I've set up a sugar-water feeder in my backyard, and from my study window I watch ruby-throated hummingbirds hover and dart. On long trips in the car, I drive my family crazy scanning highway trees for hawks and owls.

My passion for birds started when I was nine with a pet parakeet named Magoo. I'd let Magoo perch on my finger and hold him up to my face while he pecked salt off my nose. I think it was this early face-to-face encounter with Magoo's beak that got me thinking about bird beaks.

I cannot live without birds. I can't go outside without watching for them, and marveling at the beauty and variety of their beaks. In fact, the words for *Unbeatable Beaks* poured out of me after I spotted a woodpecker chiseling a hole in a neighbor's tree. So, the next time you're outside, I urge you to look for birds—and their amazing, unbeatable beaks.

Ask any spoonbill, crossbill, emu, cockatoo,
mockingbird, magpie,
avocet, or parakeet—

ROSEATE SPOONBILL

WHITE-WINGED
CROSSBILL

ORANGE-FRONTED
PARAKEET

EMU

The neatest thing
besides two feet,
without question,
is a beak.

SADDLE-BILLED
STORK

GREATER FLAMEBACK

Bird beaks chisel, bird beaks hook,
bird beaks give the birds the look.

DOUBLE-CRESTED
CORMORANT

Pickax, rolling pin, fishing net, straw,
sledgehammer, army knife, needle-point claw.

BROWN PELICAN

RAZORBILL

RHINOCEROS HORNBILL

SWORD-BILLED HUMMINGBIRD

PILEATED
WOODPECKER

GREATER AKIALOA
HONEYCREEPER

AMERICAN CROW

A beak can pry, a beak can preen,
the shape is straight,
bent,
in between.

AMERICAN WOODCOCK

MANGROVE CUCKOO

ROSEATE SPOONBILL

A beak is a spoon, a beak is a slicer.
A beak is a scraper, stabber, and spiker.

ANHINGA

Beaks come in black, pink,
white, or tan—
red, green, blue
as a wild toucan.

KEEL-BILLED TOUCAN

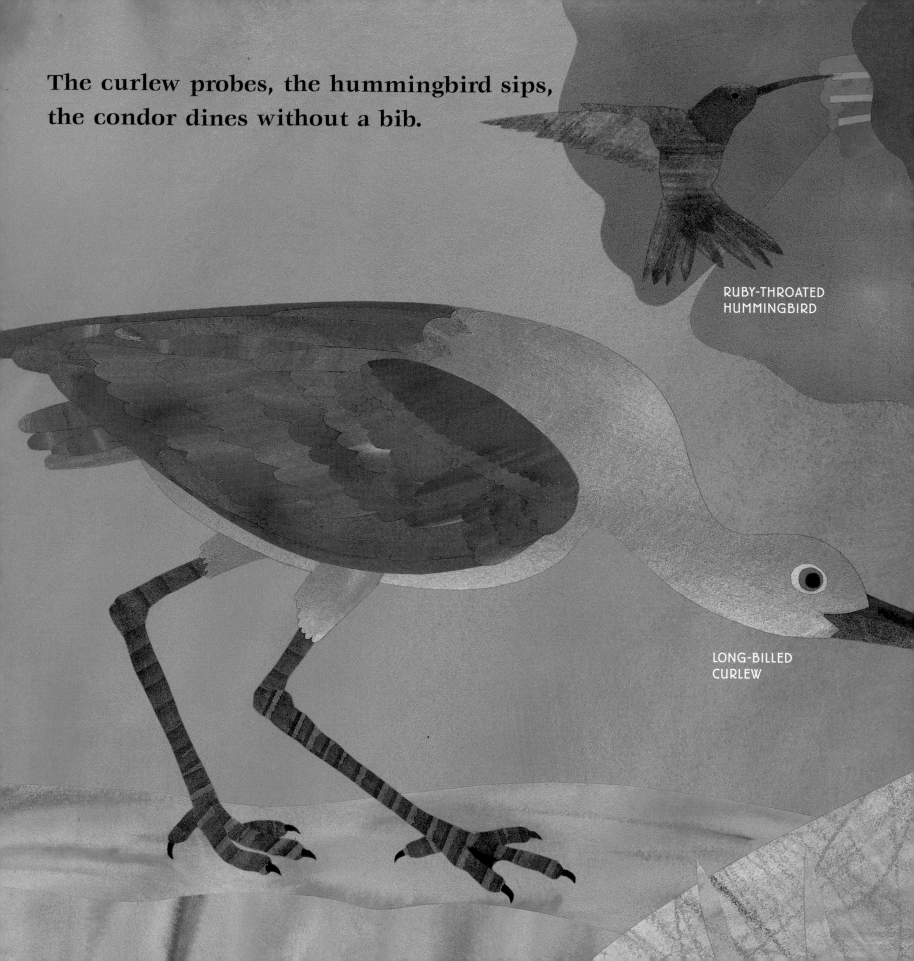

The curlew probes, the hummingbird sips,
the condor dines without a bib.

RUBY-THROATED
HUMMINGBIRD

LONG-BILLED
CURLEW

CALIFORNIA CONDOR

SNAIL KITE

Kites bite and sometimes pick.
Skimmers perform the coolest trick.

BLACK SKIMMER

Build a nest, turn an egg, climb a branch, scratch...

BALTIMORE ORIOLE

Crack a seed, pick a flea, fight a foe, hatch.

NORTHERN FLICKERS

NORTHERN
FULMAR

BOBOLINK

Ask any flamingo, fulmar,
bobolink, bufflehead,
woodpecker, whippoorwill,
pelican, puffin,
yellow-breasted chat—

BUFFLEHEAD

GREATER FLAMINGO

GREAT SPOTTED
WOODPECKER

BROWN PELICAN

YELLOW-BREASTED
CHAT

ATLANTIC PUFFIN

WHIPPOORWILL

The world's best tool
is a beak.
And that's that!

PEACH-FACED
LOVEBIRDS

Match the bird with its beak.

(You can always refer back to the birds on previous pages.)

1.

2.

3.

4.

5.

A. Puffin
B. Flamingo
C. Condor
D. Curlew
E. Spoonbill
F. Skimmer

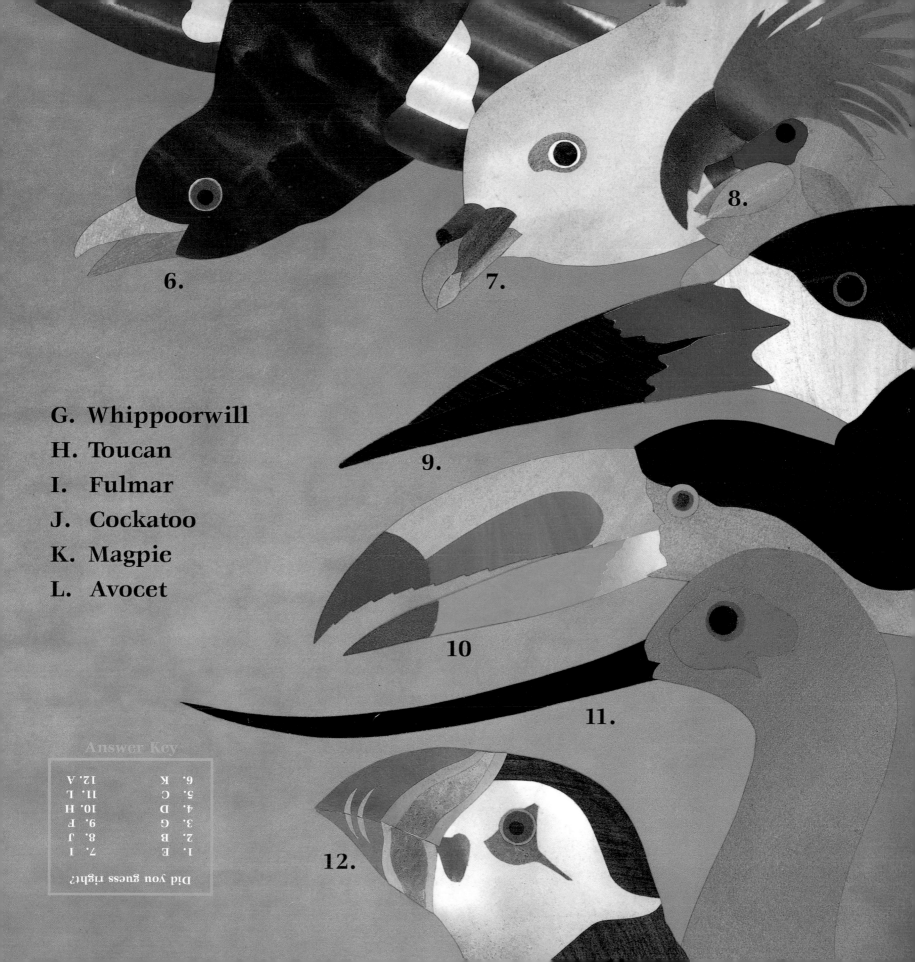

G. Whippoorwill
H. Toucan
I. Fulmar
J. Cockatoo
K. Magpie
L. Avocet

6.

7.

8.

9.

10

11.

12.

AMERICAN AVOCET   Slender, upturned beak; eats floating seeds and insects; breeds around lakes and ponds of western United States; winter visitor to the East Coast.

AMERICAN CROW   Strong, pointed beak; eats insects, fruit, bird eggs, corn, and carrion; breeds throughout the United States.

AMERICAN WOODCOCK   Long, slender beak; eats earthworms; breeds from southern Canada to Gulf states; winters in southern United States.

ANHINGA   Long, pointed beak; eats fish; lives between southeast United States and Argentina.

ATLANTIC PUFFIN   Colorful, triangular beak; eats small fish; breeds along North Atlantic coast; winters in open ocean of North Atlantic.

BALTIMORE ORIOLE   Short, pointed beak; eats insects and spiders; breeds in Canada and eastern United States; winters in Mexico and South America.

BLACK SKIMMER   Upper part of beak is short, lower part is long; eats fish; breeds along the coast from Cape Cod to South America; winters in south United States.

BOBOLINK   Short beak; eats insects in summer and grain in winter; breeds in northern United States; winters in South America.

BROWN PELICAN   Long, flat beak with huge throat pouch; eats fish; lives year-round along southern Atlantic and Pacific coasts as well as Gulf and Texas coasts of United States.

BUFFLEHEAD   Small beak; eats small insects, snails, and fish; breeds along lakes, ponds, and rivers of Alaska and Canada; winters in southern United States and Mexico.

CALIFORNIA CONDOR   Featherless head and neck; eats carrion, such as dead sheep, deer, and cattle; lives in mountains of southern California; member of vulture family.

DOUBLE-CRESTED CORMORANT   Hook-tipped beak; eats fish and crabs; breeds along coasts of North America; winters in Mexico and Bahamas.

EMU   Flightless Australian bird; eats grasses, fruit, seeds, and insects.

GREAT SPOTTED WOODPECKER   Straight, pointed beak; eats wood-boring beetles and ants; lives year-round across Europe.

GREATER AKIALOA HONEYCREEPER   Long, down-curved beak; eats insects; lives in the forests on the island of Kauai in Hawaii.

GREATER FLAMEBACK   Sharp, pointed beak; eats insects; lives in India, southwest China, and the Philippines.

GREATER FLAMINGO   Bent beak; eats small fish, insects, and crabs; breeds on Atlantic and Gulf coasts; visitor to southern Florida.

KEEL-BILLED TOUCAN   Large, colorful beak; eats mostly fruit, also insects, lizards, and eggs; lives in tropical forests from Mexico to South America.

LONG-BILLED CURLEW   Long beak; eats crabs, grasshoppers, and worms; breeds in grasslands of western United States; winters in southern marshes and coastal flats.

MANGROVE CUCKOO   Short, curved beak; eats caterpillars and other insects; lives in coastal mangroves of southern Florida, the West Indies, and Mexico.

MARSH WREN (on cover of book)   Small, pointed beak; eats insects and spiders; lives across southern Canada and northern United States; winters in southern United States.

NORTHERN FLICKER   Sharp, pointed beak; eats mostly ants; lives from Canada to southern United States.

NORTHERN FULMAR   Large, tube-nosed beak; eats fish; breeds along rocky coasts of northern Canada; winters on open seas off north Atlantic and Pacific coasts.

NORTHERN MOCKINGBIRD   Slender beak; eats insects, berries, and fruit; lives year-round across the United States.

ORANGE-FRONTED PARAKEET   Hooked beak; eats fruit, flowers, and seeds; lives year-round in Mexico and Costa Rica; visitor to East Coast states.

PALM COCKATOO   Large, powerful beak; eats palm nuts and seeds; lives in rainforests of New Guinea and northeast Australia.

PEACH-FACED LOVEBIRD   Parrotlike beak; eats fruit and berries; lives in Angola and Namibia, Africa.

PILEATED WOODPECKER   Sharp, pointed beak; eats tree-boring insects and some fruit; lives in Canada and eastern United States.

RAZORBILL   Thick, flat beak; eats fish and crabs; breeds along coastal cliffs of north Atlantic; winters on open seas of north Atlantic.

RHINOCEROS HORNBILL   Massive, thick beak; eats fruit, berries, and insects; lives in forests of Indonesia and Malaysia.

ROSEATE SPOONBILL   Spoon-shaped beak; eats fish, crabs, and insects; lives year-round along Florida and Texas coasts.

RUBY-THROATED HUMMINGBIRD   Tiny, pointed beak; sips flower nectar; lives in gardens across eastern two-thirds of the United States; winters in Mexico and Central America.

SADDLE-BILLED STORK   Large, heavy beak; eats frogs and small animals; lives in Kenya and northern Tanzania.

SNAIL KITE   Sharp, hooked beak; eats freshwater snails; breeds from Florida Everglades to South America.

SWORD-BILLED HUMMINGBIRD   Five-inch-long beak; sips flower nectar; lives in Venezuela, Colombia, Ecuador, Peru, and northern Bolivia.

WHIPPOORWILL   Small beak with wide mouth; eats moths, beetles, and other flying insects; breeds across eastern and southwestern United States; winters in southern United States.

WHITE-WINGED CROSSBILL   Top and bottom beaks cross; eats pinecone seeds; lives year-round in evergreen forests of northern United States.

YELLOW-BILLED MAGPIE   Stout beak; eats insects, fruit, and seeds; lives year-round in valleys and hills of California.

YELLOW-BREASTED CHAT   Small, slender beak; eats insects and berries; breeds throughout United States.